Top 10 Interesting Facts About Hindu Mythology and Gods

The Hindu religion is the most established religion whose beginning can be followed back to ancient occasions around 5000 to 10,000 BC. So it is no big surprise that huge numbers of the fantasies, convictions, and folklores encompassing the religion are similarly as old.

Truth be told, given this course of events, a considerable lot of these legends may have experienced various retellings throughout the years. Hindu folklore has rich history, perplexing characters, resonating stories, and a shockingly natural relationship with current science. There are likewise recurrent timeframes that recurrent themselves after a specific span. There additionally are sagas like Mahabharata and Ramayana, the previous being the longest known epic ever. Here is a rundown of the main 10 most intriguing realities about old Hindu folklore:

10. The Hindu Epics

The Hindu stories were composed to make moral beliefs for adherents to hope for. These legends were written in Sanskrit and in their quintessence portrayed the intensity of the Hindu divine beings in beautiful stanza. The most mainstream of these beautiful stories are the Ramayana and Mahabharata. The Ramayana is a sublime portrayal of the tale of Rama. It narratives the life of Rama from his introduction to the world in the realm of Ayodhya to his conclusive triumph over his abhorrent foe Ravana. The epic says a lot on the temperance of genuine fellowship, love, and the idea of penance one needs to make to vanquish fiendish.

The Mahabharata is the longest epic at any point composed and gives an inside and out knowledge into the ascent of Hinduism between 400 BC and 200 AD. Truth be told, its whole portrayal is multiple times the length of the Illiad and the Odyssey consolidated. Aside from its superb portrayal of the battle between the Kauravas and the Pandavas, it likewise subtleties the contents of the Bhagavat Gita. From start to finish, it portrays the extraordinary fight that set sibling in opposition to sibling. In time, the Bhagavat Gita proceeded to turn into the encapsulation of Hinduism's holy sacred text.

9. Treta Yuga

This speaks to the second age in the pattern of Maha Yuga. The Hindu contents express that Treta Yuga ranges a time of 1,296,000 human years. By the coming of Treta Yuga, the nearness of sattva or goodness in human instinct had gradually begun to reduce. Whatever decency or uprightness that stayed in individuals was currently joined by an ever-expanding measure of tamas and rajas. Tamas spoke to the obscurity in human instinct and rajas comprised all the energy a human could invoke. At this point, individuals had sustained an intense degree of astuteness, however they had additionally lost a decent arrangement of command over their body and its physiology.

Individuals' height was currently littler than during the Satya Yuga, with the normal individual around 14 cubits tall, however there were some uncommon creatures who had accomplished a faithful form and celestial persona, for example, the characters Rama, Laxamana, Ravana, and Hanumana who were viewed as exceptional for their phenomenal quality and incomparable mind.

8. Dwapar Yuga

Dwapar Yuga speaks to the third age directly after Treta Yuga. Otherwise called the Bronze Age, the Dwapar Yuga is said to have gone on for 864,000 human years. It speaks to an age where goodness and malice in human instinct are in a dead heat. As the human body loses satva or virtue, individuals achieve a far more noteworthy command over their body than their mind. When Dwapar Yuga was at its pinnacle, man had just lost authority over his deepest body and information.

He turned out to be more pulled in to the materialistic parts of the world, capitulating to his ever-expanding wants. Just scholarly people like Bhisma, Dharmaraja, and Vidura had the option to get away from this destiny. In the long run, there was a continuous decrease in the ethical fiber of society when all is said in done. Individuals with huge rawness turned out to be progressively hostile in their hunger for want and force. The normal human life expectancy had additionally boiled down to 1,000 years.

7. Kali Yuga

The last age in the ever-rehashing pattern of Maha Yuga is the Kali Yuga. It is likewise the most limited, going on for 432,000 human years. The present timeframe falls under Kali Yuga, and it is additionally alluded to as the Iron Age. The Kali Yuga speaks to affectation and unsteadiness more than ever.

Human instinct is fundamentally debased by the enticements of transgression and just a little still, small voice remains.

The human body is at its most reduced regarding rawness and acumen. A normal man is just 3.5 cubits tall and lives for around 100 to 120 years. Refering to the antiquated Hindu contents, it is evaluated that around 5,000 years of Kali Yuga have just cruised by. It is additionally anticipated that when Kali Yuga arrives at its withering years, the life expectancy of man will be close to 20 years. This age has been featured by man's extraordinary yearning for realism. In an unmistakable difference to past ages, human lives have been debased by numbness and the association with one's internal identity has been lost.

6. The Curses

Condemnations have a long and interesting history in a wide range of folklores. The Hindu divine beings infrequently reviled for they employed force sufficiently compelling to exact whatever enduring they wanted for other people.

Yet at the same time, there have been numerous occurrences of one of a kind reviles inside Hindu folklore that merit referencing.

In the epic Mahabharata, the Pandavas were hit by gigantic distress on acknowledging Karna was their relative from the beginning. They had quite recently murdered him in fight. A maddened Yudhisthara couldn't accept their mom Kunti would keep such close to home data from them, so he made a revile that no lady from that point on ought to have the option to leave well enough alone from others. At that point, there is the revile on the character Pandu that on the off chance that he at any point moved toward a lady with sentiments of want, he would pass on the spot.

Be that as it may, likely the most eminent revile of everything is when Gandhari reviled Lord Krishna in the outcome of the Mahabharata. In the wake of overcoming the Kauravas and executing every one of the 100 children of Gandhari, Krishna went to support a troubled mother. On observing Krishna, Gandhari reviled that nobody in Krishna's bloodline would live to see people in the future. Also, similarly as the Kauravas bloodline had been ended, the entirety of Krishna's family executed each other at the appointed time. Krishna passed on a less than ideal demise with nobody left to proceed with his bloodline.

5. The Vedas and Modern Science

The Vedas speak to an assortment of psalms and strict writings that were defined somewhere close to 1500 and 1000 BC. These holy sections were written in the Indus area where it is trusted Hinduism began. The sacred text utilized in the Vedas is Sanskrit. Despite the fact that the Vedas were made thousands out of years back, researchers have discovered a solid association between their messages and current science.

For example, present day researchers set forward the possibility of the presence of numerous universes in string hypothesis. It states we live in a multiverse — there are numerous universes that exist in equal. The Hindu Vedas plainly reverberation this "cutting edge" idea by referencing the presence of patterned endless universes in the old Hindu cosmology. The consecrated messages in the Vedas and the Bhagavad Gita were impeccable in their comprehension of the universe. Actually, Albert Einstein once stated: "When I read the Bhagavad Gita and reflect about how God made this universe everything else appears to be unnecessary."

4. Foundation of Hinduism

Hinduism is very not normal for other conventional religions. It didn't begin from a solitary originator or hallowed sacred text or at a specific point in time. Hinduism is an amalgamation of various convictions, conventions, and methods of reasoning. These various perspectives are as a rule at chances with one another. So normally, there are various hypotheses on the starting point of the world's most established religion. Its first notice can be followed back to the most punctual compositions of old Hindu sages or Rishis. Be that as it may, once more, even these holy works were initially articulated orally.

The most punctual hints of practices that took after Hindu customs can be followed back to old India around 5500 BC. It is muddled on the off chance that these conventions had a particular terminology back, at that point. The expression "Hindu" began uniquely during the Mughal time in contemporary India. Hinduism turned into a mainstream reference just during the nineteenth and twentieth hundreds of years, when English frontier rule saw fast development in India. Proof likewise shows that a plain god named Siva was prevalently venerated by the Indus Valley human progress around 3000 BC. The best all things considered, the Mahabharata, was composed somewhere close to 400 BC and 200 AD, and it gave a massive understanding into Hindu folklore as the Bhagavad Gita alongside other truly significant writings.

3. Satya Yuga

Hindu folklore obviously expresses that every single living being go through a nonstop pattern of creation and obliteration, the Maha Yuga. This cycle rehashes itself more than four distinctive ages or Yugas. The first of these Yugas is the Satya Yuga, which traverses a time of 1,728,000 years. The Satya Yuga is supposed to be the brilliant time of truth and edification. In this age, individuals accomplished a perfect perspective and their activities were constantly contemplated and upright. The consecrated messages further express that there was an overflow stream of thoughts and contemplations between individuals.

Everybody drove a genuine life and clung to reality. Everybody had obtained the response to a definitive inquiry – the starting point of everything. What's more, since there was basically nothing to hide, even the littlest string of thought was available to everybody without verbal correspondence. Human physiology likewise essentially contrasted from the one that we show today. Individuals used to be around 31.5 feet (21 cubits or 80cm) tall. They likewise had a life expectancy that extended more than a huge number of years.

2. Gods and Goddesses

Hinduism follows a polytheistic convention. Hindus love different gods, and these divine beings and goddesses as a rule have a place with a specific pantheon of divinities. Truth be told, refering to specific lines in the holy Hindu contents, many accept that there are around 330 million divine beings in Hindu folklore. Every one of these divine beings and goddesses represent a specific part of life. For instance, the goddess Saraswati is the wellspring of all information and insight and the god Brahma is the maker of reality as we probably am aware it. Truth be told, the celestial trinity of Brahma, Vishnu, and Shiva is viewed as a reason for the entire of Hindu folklore.

Be that as it may, the Vedas obviously state there are just 33 significant gods. The progress into 300 million divine beings came during the Upanishadic age trying to mirror the limitless idea of the universe. Regardless of such huge quantities of divine beings and goddesses, Hindus are essentially committed to a solitary god. The various divine beings are taken as various symbols (features) of their essential god. Regarding age, all the essential divinities are as old as time and creation itself.

1. Theory of Creation

Hindu folklore gives a few records of how precisely the formation of the universe occurred. The appropriate responses themselves go into fluctuating degrees of intricacy since there have been various methodologies at various occasions. Maybe the most well known methodology expresses that the most noteworthy divinities were unmindful of their own quality before the presence of time itself. Prior to creation, there was no time, no paradise or earth, or space in the middle. There was just the dim sea that washed into the shores of nothingness.

In another delineation, everything began with the articulation of a consecrated sound, oom (aum).

Old Hindu sacred texts express that a definitive reality (Brahman) has three principle capacities. These three qualities are found in the trinity of divine beings: Brahma, Vishnu, and Shiva. That is the reason we can see pictures where the leaders of the trinity are consolidated into a solitary body called the Trimurti. In the Trimurti, Brahma is the maker of everything, Vishnu is the preserver of nature, and Shiva is a definitive destroyer who achieves change at whatever point it gets vital.

Conclusion

Hinduism is viewed as the most seasoned religion on the planet. In any case, it is considerably more than that. Hindu folklore has been lenient of different religions and conventions since its commencement. Regarding sacred writing, it is a brilliant mixture of epic accounts of profound quality and honorableness. These accounts give us perfect characters like Rama, Laxamana, and the Pandavas. The Vedas give us an understanding into antiquated science and stargazing. Sagas like Mahabharata and Ramayana describe divine accounts of the endless fight among great and malice. These are the reasons that the rich history of Hindu folklore is captivating for the two Hindus and non-Hindus.

Top 10 Hindu Gods

Religion is a declaration of mankind's quest for a total image of the universe. The inalienable want to comprehend the world, karma, presence, and time is a significant purpose for religion and an individual's love of a preeminent being. Hinduism is probably the most established religion on the planet and furthermore the third biggest. There are numerous divine beings and goddesses in Hinduism; their definite number can't be discovered. While various types of divinities are loved, it is accepted that all aficionados are really loving one preeminent being

10. Indra

Indra is the ruler of paradise and the pioneer of the Devas. He is the divine force of downpour. Airavat, a propitious trinket, is his vehicle or vahan. Another of his vehicles is a chariot drawn by 10,000 ponies. His weapon, speaking to both a precious stone and a thunderclap, is known as the vajra. He is the child of Aditi and the sage Kashyap. Indra is one of the most significant divinities, regularly appeared as a cleverness god, sending snags in the method of enthusiasts, particularly the Asuras with the point of destroying individuals' endeavors to satisfy the divine beings. Indra represents quality and fortitude.

9. Hanuman

Hanuman, otherwise called the monkey god, is the child of the air god, Pawan or Vayu. He is additionally one of the eight immortals known as the Astachiranjiwi. It is accepted that a youthful Hanuman once attempted to swallow the sun. Because of his devilish nature, his forces were limited until he met Ram. In the wake of meeting Ram, Hanuman turned into a dependable lover assuming a focal job in the epic Ramayana. He was probably the most grounded partner who torched Lanka (the incredible ruler Ravan's realm). Hanuman is broadly associated with sparing Ram's sibling Lakshman via conveying a whole heap of sanjiwani buti, an actual existence sparing herb. For every one of these reasons, he is the image of the intensity of commitment.

8. Harihara

Harihara is the consolidated epitome of two incomparable Hindu divinities. Hari represents Vishnu and Hara represents Shiva. In view of this combination, Harihara is trailed by the two enthusiasts of Vishnu and Shiva as the type of the incomparable god. Harihara in this manner shows the significance of all divine beings as a definitive force known to man. The iconography of Harihara is part into equal parts. One half speaks to Shiva holding the trishul, a drum, and a deer. The other half speaking to Vishnu has the conch shell and chakra.

7. Kumar Kartikeya

Kumar is a Hindu warrior god. He is additionally known by the names Kumar Kartikeya or Kartikeya. He is the principal child of Shiva and Parvati. One of the significant goals of his introduction to the world was to murder the evil presence Tarkasur. Along these lines, he was raised by the Kirtikas, far away from his folks to shield him from Tarkasur's endeavors to execute him. Subsequent to accomplishing his forces, Kumar was designated as the president of the Devas in the fight against Tarkasur. Because of his mental fortitude and expertise, Kumar was offered the situation of the ruler of paradise, however he turned this down as he thought about his job as the president to be increasingly significant. His vehicle is the peacock.

6. Krishna

Krishna, likewise known by the names Shri Krishna, Vasudeva, Govinda, Gopal, and Madhusudan, is the eighth manifestation of Vishnu and one of the most commended scholars and warriors in Hinduism. He was the child of Basudev and Devaki. He was bound to slaughter his barbarous uncle Kansa, King of Mathura. He was raised by his non-permanent parents Yashoda and Nanda in Gokul to guard him from his uncle's dangerous endeavors. The celebration Krishna Janmastami is commended to stamp his introduction to the world. Krishna is additionally one of the focal figures in the epic Mahabharata. In the Battle of Kurukshetra, he pledged not to utilize any weapon, however offered to be Arjuna's chariot rider. It was during this fight Arjuna was confronted with the difficulty of battling against his family, and Krishna gave him the information on the Gita to help.

5. Ram

Sri Ram or Ram, the oldest child of Kaushalya and Dasharatha and leader of the Ayodhya realm, is the seventh manifestation of Vishnu. He is otherwise called Ramchandra/Rama. The celebration of Ram Nawami is commended to check his introduction to the world. Smash is the focal hero of the epic Ramayana. Kaikeyi, one of his stepmothers, needed him ousted so her child could be the following lord, so Ram was sent into banish with his significant other Sita and sibling Lakshman for a long time. Devoured by underhanded wants and desire, Ravan, the King of Lanka, kidnapped Sita during their outcast. This in the long run prompted the war during which Ram crushed Ravan.

4. Ganesh

Ganesh, the elephant god, is one of the most significant Hindu gods. He is the second child of Shiva and Parvati, and Kumar's more youthful sibling. While playing out any puja or custom, he is the main god to be venerated. Because of a misconception where Shiva didn't realize that Ganesh was his child, he remove Ganesh's head out of frustration. Afterward, an elephant's head was put on Ganesh and he was restored, likewise being allowed the intensity of the primary god arranged by significance. Mushak, the mouse, is his vehicle. Ganesh is regularly connected with Mangal or Mars, and good karma.

3. Vishnu

Vishnu, the defender of the universe, is one of the trinity divine forces of Hinduism alongside Brahma and Mahesh. He is otherwise called Narayan and Hari. Before the universe was made, Vishnu is accepted to have been sleeping in a huge ocean of nothingness. Vishnu is well known for his manifestations known as symbols. Being the defender of the universe, his manifestations are liable for shielding the world from malicious powers and maintaining harmony and control. Vishnu has manifested multiple times. Individuals accept that his tenth manifestation, Kalki, will approach the apocalypse. Garuda, the legendary fowl, is his vehicle. Vishnu dwells in Vishnuloka.

2. Brahma

Brahma, additionally one of the trinity divine forces of Hinduism, is the maker of the universe. He is regularly depicted as the four-headed god, speaking to four bearings. It is accepted that Brahma in certainty had five heads. Due to the pride of the fifth head, it was cut off by Shiva. While Brahma himself is the maker of the universe, he developed from the lotus bloom in the navel of Vishnu. The swan or goose is his vehicle. Brahma dwells in Brahmaloka.

1. Mahesh (Shiva)

Mahesh, the destroyer of the universe, is likewise one of the trinity lords of Hinduism. He is prominently known as Shiva, Ashutosh, and Mahadev. He is the main god in the trinity who lives on Earth at Kailash. Mahesh is appeared as a caring spouse and father, and a yogi in his kind structures, while in his savage exemplifications he is viewed as the destroyer, killing evil spirits and Asurs. Shiva, additionally the watchman divine force of contemplation, yoga, and craftsmanship, is beautified with the consecrated stream, the Ganga and the peaceful moon, the Chandra, on his head. He is viewed as an exceptionally straightforward god loved as Lingam.

Conclusion

Divine beings in Hinduism can be dissected as a lot of useful gods, the trinity being the most famous. Every god holds a particular reason and force. For instance, Indra is the downpour god; Kumar is the president; the trinity divine beings are the maker, defender, and destroyer; and others speak to various practical parts of the divine beings. Contingent upon the time and spot, the ubiquity of the gods may differ. While their appearances and forces might be extraordinary, every one of them assume a significant job in the creation, security, pulverization, and continuation of the universe.